So Scandalous

Book Six of the Bex Carter Series

Tiffany Nicole Smith

Contact me. I'd love to hear from you!

authortiffanynicole@gmail.com

Twitter @Tigerlilly79

Cover Designed by

Keri Knutson @ Alchemy Book Covers

So Scandalous

Book 6 of the Bex Carter Series

by

Tiffany Nicole Smith

Countdown to Australia!

There are ninety-seven days until I get to go to Australia with my super-cool aunt. I've been keeping up my grades and writing in my journal as part of our agreement. I hope nothing ruins our trip!

1

Scandalous

#stoptherumors

I'm only in the eighth grade, but my life is like a soap opera, full of drama and mystery. The problem with that is I've always hated soap operas. I'd never known how my nana could watch those things. Anyway, it seems that everywhere I turn, I'm faced with some secret, scandal, or juicy gossip. There's a lot going on at Lincoln Middle right now, and yours truly seems to be right in the middle of it.

The drama started on Sunday afternoon when I found out my aunt Jeanie had lied to me. She'd always told me that I could be open with her and tell her anything, and she would understand. That was *so* not true. I told her that I was going out with someone (yes, I have a boyfriend; I know, right?), and she totally flipped out. She didn't know what to do, so she called my aunt Alice over for advice.

I love Aunt Alice to pieces. She's one of my best friends, but when she came, she only made things worse.

That afternoon Santiago (my B.F.) and I sat side by side on the living room couch while my aunts stared at us as if we were some kind of weird scientific specimens.

Aunt Jeanie shook her head. "I'm not okay with this. She's just too young to be dating."

Aunt Alice looked from me to Santiago. "Jeanie, she's thirteen—"

"Uh, I'm fourteen."

"But I'm thirteen," Santiago said. "Hey, I'm dating an older woman. Cool."

I nudged him in the ribs with my elbow. He was totally not helping.

"Right, fourteen," Aunt Alice said. "We all had boyfriends at that age. It's nothing serious. Just puppy love."

"I know, I know, but it's already hard for Bex to focus and keep her grades up. I don't want Sanchez to distract her."

"Santiago," I said, correcting my aunt.

"Right, Santiago."

"If you ban her from having a boyfriend," Aunt Alice continued, "she's just going to do it behind your back.

They'll still see each other at school and other places only you won't know about it. Right, Bex?"

"Uh . . ." Seriously, how was I supposed to answer that question?

They went on and on and on, arguing with each other as if we weren't even there, and throughout the course of their conversation, Santiago was called Sanchez (again) San Diego, and San Jose. I finally stopped correcting my aunt.

I don't know what I had expected from Aunt Jeanie. I'd figured I would say, "Hey, remember when you said to be open with you? Well, I'm going out with my friend Santiago." And then she would go, "Oh, Bex, I'm so happy for you. I'm glad to see that you finally have a boyfriend."

Really, I was the only one in my group of friends who had never had a boyfriend-boyfriend.

But that Sunday afternoon as I sat there, mortified, I wondered if Santiago would break up with me on the spot and run out of the house screaming because of my crazy family. By the time Aunt Alice left, I still wasn't sure if Aunt Jeanie was going to let me go out with Santiago. She said that she had to sleep on it.

I asked her for her answer the following morning. She told me to get out of her bedroom because it was 4 AM. I knew it was super-early, but I needed to know if I had a boyfriend or not, and the suspense was killing me.

What happened on Sunday was nothing compared to what happened on Monday. After Social Studies, I had to go to the restroom really bad, so I made a mad dash to the girls' room in the social studies wing.

Unfortunately, all the stalls were full except for the one at the end—the cursed stall. The door of the cursed stall is white, while the rest are beige, and legend has it that anyone who uses that stall will fail all their classes and have to repeat their grade. For a second, I wondered if I could wait it out, but there was no way I could hold it.

Once I had done my business, I looked up to see large red letters written sloppily on the door of the stall.

"Piper Benson stuffs her bra?" I read aloud.

I heard a gasp from outside of the stall. "What? No way."

I looked through the crack of the stall and saw a flash of strawberry blond hair and a familiar hot pink puffer vest. Miranda Phillips, Lincoln Middle's very own news reporter. The girl was a walking gossip column. Everything that came out of her mouth was someone else's business.

"I knew it!" Miranda said. "Winter growth spurt, my foot! I knew she was lying!"

"No, wait!" I yelled as I buckled my belt. "I was just reading—"

"I can't wait to tell Bethany."

I heard the bathroom door open and close.

After that, I didn't think much of the incident, but I should have. Who knew that five little words scribbled on the door of a cursed bathroom stall could cause so much trouble?

By lunchtime, Piper Benson was in tears because kids had been walking by, sneezing, and asking her for tissues all morning. Her friends had vowed to find the person who started such an awful rumor. I guess that might have been me, but I hadn't written it; I'd only read it aloud. How was I supposed to know that the biggest mouth in the state was standing right outside of the door?

I wanted to tell them the truth, that someone had written the rumor on the door of the bathroom stall, but then this happened:

Piper's best friend, Kristen Lee stood on the bench of their lunch table. "Whoever started this rumor is going to regret it. When I find out who it was, they are going to wish they were never born. You might as well transfer right now!"

One of the lunch monitors yelled at her to sit down and be quiet. She did, glaring.

Normally I wouldn't have been afraid of such a threat, but Kristen Lee was ruthless, and I'd already had a run-in with her. By "run-in", I mean a real, physical fight, and I had no intentions on going there with her again—mainly because she has a black belt in karate and a mean drop kick. If I admitted that I had (accidentally) started the rumor, everyone would hate me and treat me like some sort of criminal.

After the lunch bell rang, I quietly caught up with Miranda. "You know, I happened to be in the bathroom earlier, and someone wrote that rumor about Piper on the wall of the stall."

Miranda's hazel eyes grew wide, and she grabbed my arm. "Show me. Maybe I can recognize the handwriting." Then she leaned in close to me. "And it's not a rumor—she has totally been stuffing her bra."

I led Miranda to the very last stall of the girls' room. Natasha Del Rio was just coming out when we got there. She was kind of new to the school, and maybe she hadn't heard about the cursed stall yet.

I opened the door and discovered, much to my surprise, that the words were gone.

What was even more surprising was that new words were there, in the same red ink and messy handwriting: *Kristen Lee stole her new charm bracelet from the Lincoln Town Mall.*

Kristen had been bragging about that bracelet since her parents had given it to her for her birthday. Almost every girl had wanted one just like it.

"No way," Miranda said. "Wait until everyone hears this."

"You don't even know if it's true or not."

She took out her phone. "Oh, if it's written in the stall of the bathroom, it's true. Trust me."

"What? How do you figure? Anyone could have written that."

The bell rang, letting us know that we were late for fifth period.

Miranda pulled me out of the bathroom. "Whoever wrote that is obviously afraid of Kristen, so they wanted to be anonymous. I knew that girl was a lot of things, but a thief?"

Miranda was already texting away. By the time school was dismissed, everyone would know that Kristen Lee was a thief, whether she was one or not.

2

My Friend Who Happens to Be a Boy

—not in a relationship ☹

Journal Entry #12

Just when I think Aunt Jeanie can't ruin my life any more than she already has, she manages to find a way to do it. Sometimes it feels like she just doesn't want me to be happy. What have I ever done to her?

It had been a rough day, but when I got home from school, it got even worse. Aunt Jeanie called me to her bedroom, where one of her many parenting books lay on the bed.

"Sit down, Bex," she said, patting the bed beside her.

I took a deep breath and sat down, preparing myself for what she was going to tell me.

"Your Uncle Bob and I have decided—"

Translation: "I told Uncle Bob our decision—"

"You are just too young to have a boyfriend right now."

I knew it! "But that's not fair. Everybody else my age is dating."

"But you're not everybody else," Aunt Jeanie and I said at the same time, because I knew exactly what she was going to say.

I suddenly wished that I hadn't even told her about Santiago.

She took my hand and squeezed. "I have to do what's best for you, and right now, I just think you're too young to date. Sanchez is still welcome to come over, and you can go places when your uncle Bob and I are there, but he can't be your boyfriend."

That sounded like the worst arrangement ever. Who wants to go on a date with Aunt Jeanie?

But I learned a long time ago that there was no use arguing with Aunt Jeanie. She always won.

"Fine," I said before going to my room to mope. I called one of my best friends, Lily-Rose, because she would understand. She had been dating our friend Maverick for a long time, and her parents had no idea. They were super-strict, and she wasn't allowed to have a boyfriend, either.

"Bex, I'm sorry, but this isn't a deal-breaker. There are so many ways around the no-boyfriend rule. You'd be surprised how many girls we know aren't allowed to date yet, but they manage."

"Really? How?" I asked.

"Just think about it. You can still hang out at school. Santiago can still come over. You guys can still hang out. Just tell your aunt you're meeting friends. It's not really a lie."

It seemed a little sneaky, but being honest had put me in this position in the first place.

"The only difference," Lily-Rose said, "is that you can't call him your boyfriend in front of your aunt. Is that really a big deal?"

She was absolutely right. What Aunt Jeanie said really wouldn't change anything.

I felt one hundred times better. I mean, this was the first time that I truly liked a boy who liked me back, and he liked me enough to want to be my boyfriend. Sometimes you had to be willing to make sacrifices for love, so not telling Aunt Jeanie the whole truth was justified. Right?

That night I told Santiago what Aunt Jeanie had said. "I don't care, Bex. I'll take whatever I can get. Even if I have to go on a date with your aunt there and listen to her call me Sanchez all night."

Isn't he the sweetest?

"What does your mom have to say about it?" I asked.

"She thinks it's cute that I have a girlfriend, and she says that I better be a perfect gentleman or she'll string me up."

I couldn't help but think that boys had it so much easier than girls when it came to these types of things. There was nothing like hanging out with my friends, but Santiago was so easy to talk to. I was about to tell him how the whole rumor about Piper had gotten started when there was a knock on my bedroom door.

Before I could even say "Who is it?" or "Come in," Aunt Jeanie had let herself in. I don't think she understands why you should knock on someone's door.

"Aunt Jeanie, what if I were changing or something?"

She rolled her eyes. "As if I haven't seen it all. Who are you talking to?"

"Chirpy," I lied.

She frowned, and I was a little afraid, because sometimes Aunt Jeanie could be a lie detector. "Well, it's getting late. Finish your homework and get to bed."

"Okay," I said. I waited for her to leave, but she didn't. I sighed and put the phone back to my ear. "Chirpy, I guess I'll see you tomorrow."

"All right," Santiago said, sounding sad. He always sounded that way when we had to hang up. "See you tomorrow."

I hung up, and a satisfied Aunt Jeanie finally left. Having a boy who was a friend was going to be harder than I thought.

3

Lincoln Middle's
Most Wanted

#sooverit

Another rumor was discovered in the girls' room the following day. I didn't find this one, since I had decided that it was best for me to stay out of that particular bathroom all together.

Ava Groves had a nose job last summer.

I had to admit that I laughed a little at that one. Ava Groves and I had never been on good terms, but I was particularly upset with her for having a hand in my heart getting broken for a second time. I'll tell you about that later.

So yeah, I didn't care much for Ava Groves before, but now, I could barely stand to look at her.

The worst part of it is that my aunt and her mother are constantly trying to push us to be friends, because they're best friends. Aunt Jeanie really wants me to be like Ava, but she has no idea how horrible she really is.

Everyone stared at Ava as we passed her in the hallway.

"I knew she was too perfect to be real," I heard a girl whisper.

"So is it true?" a sixth-grade boy asked Ava. "Do you keep your old nose in a jar or something?"

Bad move, kid.

She shoved him into a locker. "Of course, it's not true. I'm a natural beauty."

Yes, Ava was a very pretty girl, with jet-black hair and sparkling green eyes, but that was easy to forget because her attitude was so awful.

"So, what do you think?" my friend Chirpy asked as she walked beside me. I had to look down on her, since she was so short that I towered over her.

"It's not true. Thirteen-year-olds can't get plastic surgery."

Chirpy shook her head. "I don't know. When you have enough money, you can do anything. You should know."

The Groves were very well-off, and so were my aunt Jeanie and uncle Bob, but Chirpy was wrong. I wasn't rich; they were.

"Who do you think keeps writing that stuff in the bathroom?" I asked.

Chirpy shrugged. "I have no idea. Obviously someone who likes to stir up trouble. I'm not mad at them, though. Ava and Kristen totally deserve it."

While it was always nice to see mean girls get a taste of their own medicine, I had a nagging feeling that this Phantom Rumor Starter was going to cause an eighth-grade catastrophe.

By lunchtime, another rumor had been scribbled in the stall of a different bathroom. Apparently, the Phantom-Rumor-Starter wanted to switch things up. This time, the wall read:

Paisley Thomas and Roger Caldwell are secretly dating.

The rumor wouldn't have been so bad if Paisley and Roger weren't actually dating other people. Roger's girlfriend totally believed the rumor and dumped him in the hallway on front of everyone.

I felt bad for him. Why did people believe rumors so easily?

I spotted Santiago talking to Roger after school. As I approached, Santiago patted him on the shoulder, and he walked away.

"How's Roger?" I asked.

Santiago stared after him. "Miserable."

"That's too bad."

"He told me that he wants to find whoever's doing this and teach them a lesson, and that gave me a great idea."

I wasn't surprised. "What's that?"

Santiago was always thinking of ways to make money. He's been running a website design service for a few years. Other than that, he's had a bully protection service, a dating service, a babysitting service, and probably a few other things that I can't recall.

He took my hand. "I'm going to open a detective service and find out who's writing those rumors."

I couldn't help but laugh. "Santiago, what do you know about being a detective?"

"It can't be that hard. I just have to find the clues and look for evidence. If I can solve the mystery of whoever's writing these rumors, the kids might hire me to solve other things."

I thought the idea was absolutely ridiculous, but I couldn't tell him that. If he wanted to try to find out who the culprit was, what could it hurt?

Paisley Thomas came running out of the school building, with Jordan Brewster right on her heels, calling after her.

"I never want to see you again!" she screamed.

"Can you believe that everyone's just believing these lies?" Santiago asked. "I mean, how gullible can they be?"

He was right. Kids were eating these rumors like sour apple lollipops. Whether they were true or not, it was as if people wanted to believe them. It gave them something to talk about.

So far, I had seen girls crying and two perfectly good relationships break up over what had been written in the stall of the bathroom. Maybe Santiago's detective service was a good idea, after all. I hoped he would be able to get to the bottom of things before anyone else got hurt.

4

The Nightmare Next Door

—feeling spooked ☹

As if I didn't have enough going on with the non-boyfriend and the Phantom-Rumor-Starter situation, a new family was moving in next door. An elderly couple had lived there, but they had decided to downsize and buy a condo in Florida. A new family was moving in, and Aunt Jeanie was being nosey as usual.

"Their last name is Silverstein," Aunt Jeanie said as she watched them from the window.

Silverstein? That sounded familiar. Whose last name was Silverstein?

"Oh, Bex. They have a daughter. And she looks to be about your age."

"Oh, goody," I muttered. That didn't make me excited at all. I had no friends in this neighborhood. Most of the kids went to a fancy private school and haven't given me the time of day since I moved in with my aunt.

"Let's go over and say hello," Aunt Jeanie called.

"I can't. I'm in the middle of doing my homework," I called from the dining room table.

"You are not. You're doodling that boy's name in your notebook."

Busted. How did she know that? Was she psychic?

I'd always told myself that I wouldn't be one of those girl's wasting perfectly good paper writing some boy's name over and over, but there I was, doing just that. I slammed my notebook shut. "Fine."

"Sophia, the muffins, please," Aunt Jeanie called.

A moment later, Sophia, the housekeeper, came into the living room, carrying a basket of muffins and handed them to Aunt Jeanie.

As we crossed our lawn and entered the neighbor's driveway, I noticed a man and woman directing several men as they removed furniture from the moving truck. The couple stopped as we approached.

"Yoo-hoo," Aunt Jeanie called. "Welcome to the neighborhood."

The adults shook hands and Aunt Jeanie introduced us. "I'm Jeanie Maloney. I live next door. This is my niece, Rebecca, but she goes by Bex."

The man and woman looked me over. "Hello," the woman said. "Nice to meet you. I'm Adelaine Silverstein, and this is Douglas."

"You have to meet our daughter, Bex," Mrs. Silverstein said. "We were worried that there would be no kids her age in the neighborhood, and there's one right next door." She turned toward the house and called, "Sherry!"

Sherry. Sherry Silverstein! The name slapped me square in the face. Sherry Silverstein was a girl who went to my school. Everyone called her Scary Sherry, and for good reason.

A thin girl with pasty white skin, thin jet-black hair that hung in her face, and a long black dress stepped on the porch. She paused and then made her way over to us.

"Hi, Bex." Her voice was monotone, and she didn't smile.

She's always like that. That, coupled with the facts that she's as quiet as a mouse and manages to sneak up on people all the time—she had earned her nickname.

"You two know each other?" Aunt Jeanie asked, less than impressed by Sherry's appearance.

"Yes, Scar—Sherry goes to my school. She even helped me out during the election."

Sherry *had* been a part of my campaign team when I ran for eighth-grade president, but before that, I'd had very little interaction with her. We definitely weren't friends.

"Well, isn't that nice?" Aunt Jeanie said before she and the adults floated over to the moving truck. The Silversteins continued to direct the movers while Aunt Jeanie tried to get a look at their stuff. From what I could see, a lot of it was old and antique looking—the kinds of things you might see in a haunted house.

Sherry and I stood in awkward silence. She stared at the ground while her hair completely covered her face. I wanted to push her hair behind her ears.

I struggled to find something to say. "So, you're moving in right next door. That's cool. It's a really nice house."

"Yeah," Sherry said.

"Um, maybe you could come over sometime, after you guys get settled in."

"Sure," Sherry said quietly. She looked back at the house.

"Can I see your room?" I asked.

She finally looked up, almost as if she was afraid. "Um—my room? No, no it's not ready yet. Listen, Bex, I should get back to unpacking. I'll talk to you later." She ran back toward the house.

What was up with that? Instead of treating her like some kind of weirdo, like the other kids did, I was trying to be nice to her, and she was running away from me like I had the cooties.

Whatever.

I pried Aunt Jeanie away from the Silversteins. I think they were relieved, because she had been asking them fifty million questions.

"What do you think?" Aunt Jeanie whispered as we walked back to the house.

"I don't know." I wasn't sure how to take Sherry, at that point.

"They seem nice but a little strange. Their design taste is definitely gothic mixed with a little medieval—"

I tuned Aunt Jeanie out while she went on and on about their black furniture and an unusual amount of candelabras.

I looked back at the house. Sherry was standing on the porch, staring at us. I waved at her, but she didn't wave back. Weird.

5

The Sky Is Falling!

—feeling annoyed ☹

Journal Entry #13

Have you ever heard the story of Chicken Little? In a nutshell, it's a story about a chicken who gets hit in the head with an acorn or something. Immediately he assumes that the sky is falling and runs around getting everyone all frightened and panicked. That pretty much sums up what is going on at Lincoln Middle.

"No way," Chirpy said as she bit into her hot dog. "Say it ain't so."

"It is so," I told Chirpy. "I'm living right next door to Scary Sherry."

"How did you sleep last night?" asked my friend Marishca. "I would have been terrified. I heard zat she's zee ghost of a girl who died over one hundred years ago and she's come back to get revenge on zose who have wronged her."

That was about the last thing I needed to hear at that moment. There were many rumors swirling around Scary Sherry, but most of them were ridiculous. Of course Sherry wasn't a ghost. She was just . . . different. Right?

Just then, Ava squeezed herself between Santiago and me.

"Hey!" I shouted, annoyed that she had separated us. "You never sit with us. What are you doing here?"

"Is it true? I mean, really true about Scary Sherry?"

I rolled my eyes. "If you're talking about her moving next door to me, then yes. So what?"

Ava put her hands over her heart as if she were having chest pains. "OMG, I am never coming to your house again."

I squeezed more ketchup onto my French fries. "That would be awesome."

"What are you going to do?" Ava asked.

"What do you mean? What am I going to do about what?"

She leaned in closer as if she was going to whisper, but she spoke so loud that she almost burst my eardrums. "They moved because they're hiding from the law. I'm not sure what they've done, but it's something major."

Lily-Rose laughed. "Ava, people who are running from the law don't move to a house twenty minutes away. They'd leave the state or the country."

Ava scowled at her, realizing how silly she had sounded. "Anyways, Bex. I'm only trying to look out for you."

"You are not. You're just trying to be nosey. And you shouldn't be saying that about Sherry's family. Haven't you learned your lesson about how harmful rumors can be, Schnoz?"

She covered her nose with her hand. "Don't you dare call me that, Rebecca Carter." She stood to leave. "Don't say I didn't warn you." She did her famous hair flip and stalked off.

The Phantom-Rumor-Starter (or P.R.S.) had struck again. A rumor was discovered in the bathroom between third and fourth periods.

Willow Marks eats meat.

That rumor might not be a big deal to the average person, but it was a big deal to Willow. Since the fourth grade, she had prided herself on being a strict vegetarian. She had started a vegetarian club at school and was always trying to get the cafeteria to stop serving meat. Willow took her stance on not eating meat very seriously. That day, she was even wearing a shirt that read, "Eat beans, not beings."

I hadn't seen Willow since the rumor started, but I'd heard through the grapevine that she was devastated. How was she going to get kids to become vegetarians if they thought she was a hypocrite? Whoever was writing these nasty lies about people needed to be stopped.

After school, I went to find Santiago, to see how he was coming along with his investigation. I spotted him talking to a kid named Gerald in front of his locker. Santiago was scribbling something on a pad, and Gerald looked highly upset.

"What's going on?" I asked.

"Hey, Bex," Santiago said. "Gerald here just hired me to find out who stole his iPod from his locker. Since he's my first customer, he's getting a fifty-percent discount."

Gerald handed Santiago a ten-dollar bill. "If you can't find out who took it, I get my money back, right?"

Santiago patted him on the shoulder. "Of course, buddy, but I know I'm going to find this iPod thief, so don't even worry about that."

Gerald, looking satisfied, walked away.

Santiago sniffed the ten-dollar bill and slid it into his pocket. "I love the smell of money."

"I know you do. Are you any closer to finding out who's starting the rumors?"

Santiago flipped back a few pages in his notepad. "This is what I know so far. The rumors are being written in the girl's bathroom, so it has to be a girl."

I waited for the rest. "And? Is that all you came up with? Everybody already knows that."

"Hey, I'm new at this, and I'm just getting warmed up. I'm kind of at a disadvantage, because I can't go into the girls' room to actually see the evidence—but you, on the other hand . . ."

I sighed. "What do you want me to do, Santiago?"

"Just take some pictures of the writing with your phone. I've been studying how to analyze handwriting. Maybe I can tell something from it."

I nodded. "I can do that."

"Also," Santiago continued, "I want you to smell around in there."

"In the bathroom? Gross!"

"I know, but whoever's writing these rumors are cleaning them away with something a couple of hours later. I need to know what it is. That might be a clue."

I so was not doing that. "Okay, I'll call you later. I have to get home."

"Okay," Santiago said, and we looked at each other awkwardly. He held his arms out as if he was going to hug me, but then he thought better of it. He held his hand out, and I shook it.

Hey, don't judge. We're still getting used to this boyfriend-girlfriend thing.

There was even more drama when I got home from school. A bunch of busybody ladies were gathered around Aunt Jeanie's dining room table. They stopped talking when I walked in.

"Aunt Jeanie, what's going on?"

She gave me a small smile. "Nothing, Bex. Go on up and start your homework."

I slowly made my way to the staircase, because I had to know what they were talking about.

"There are just too many strange things happening all at once," commented one woman I didn't know.

"Strange things? Like what?" I asked.

Dorothy Foster, a lady who lived down the street, spoke up. "Well for one, all the dogs have been barking nonstop. They know something is wrong. And many cats have gone missing. It's a well-known fact that animals are the first to sense danger. There's an evil lurking in this neighborhood."

An evil lurking? Seriously?

"Yes," Ms. Jillian said, "and I think we all know that it's that family of freaks who just moved in next door."

"They're not freaks," I said. "You don't even know them."

"Bex . . ." Aunt Jeanie warned.

Ms. Jillian glared at me. "Something's wrong with them. Why won't they let anyone into their house?"

I was glad when Aunt Jeanie broke in, "Can you really blame them for that, Jillian? They just moved in, and everything is probably still in boxes. They probably want to wait until they have the house looking decent."

"Perhaps, but still they're hiding something. I think I saw them carrying in a dead body."

All the woman gasped.

Looking around the dining room, I was disappointed. I'd thought that spreading silly rumors would be something that kids outgrew, but here were full-grown adults, still doing the same thing. Would the rumors ever stop?

For the rest of the week, strange things kept happening around the neighborhood, and I had to admit that it seemed like too much to be a coincidence. There had been two power outages, where every house in the two-block radius had lost power for almost an hour. The first time wasn't so bad, because it happened in the daytime, but the second time happened at night.

I was on the phone with Santiago when it happened.

"It might be them, Bex," Santiago said. "They want it to be dark when they carry out their plans."

"What plans?"

"I don't know," he said. "Whatever creepy stuff they do in the dark that they don't want anyone to see."

Then one day, there was a severe thunderstorm—only over our neighborhood. Tell me that's not weird.

The Silversteins still wouldn't let anyone into their house, and whenever a neighbor went over with a welcome gift, they only opened the door a crack and then stepped out onto the porch to talk.

Without me knowing, Aunt Jeanie invited Santiago over for Saturday dinner. If I had known, I definitely would have told him not to come. He had met my family before, but sitting around the dinner table with all of them at the same time was a different story. Also Nana and Aunt Alice were coming, and when the two of them got into the same room with Aunt Jeanie, there was always an argument.

This is how I found out that Santiago was coming over:

I was in my bedroom, lounging in my beanbag chair and watching a soccer game on TV, when Aunt Jeanie barged into my room yet again.

"You're not wearing that to dinner, are you?"

I looked down at my outfit: a yellow T-shirt and green basketball shorts. I didn't see what the problem was.

"Uh, yes."

Aunt Jeanie folded her arms across her chest. "I figured you'd want to dress up a little more, since your friend was coming over."

I sat up straight. My aunt could have been talking about anybody. "What are you talking about, Aunt Jeanie?"

"Sanchez—I invited him for dinner. Since you're going to be spending so much time with him, we should get to know him a little better."

I groaned. I really liked Santiago, and I would never want to subject someone that I really liked to my family. They were a bunch of loose cannons. Not to mention that my nana had Alzheimer's, so we never knew how she was going to behave.

"You could have told me first," I said.

Aunt Jeanie frowned. "Oh, I could have sworn that I had."

She knew good and well that she had never mentioned inviting Santiago to me, and I was surprised that he hadn't said anything to me.

"Why do I need to get dressed up? It's not like he's my boyfriend. I'm not allowed to have a boyfriend, remember?"

Aunt Jeanie did her famous one-eyebrow lift. "Fine. Look like a slob. We're having dinner at six."

Ugh. I decided to give in and change into a sundress and ballet flats.

Santiago arrived five minutes before dinner was served, and we all gathered around the table. The Triple Terrors, Aunt Jeanie's eleven-year-old triplets, were being extra annoying so I tried to block them out. My little sister, Ray was giving everyone the silent treatment because she had wanted to put on a one-girl dance recital for everyone, but Aunt Jeanie said that it would have to wait until after dinner. I actually enjoyed when Ray gave us the silent treatment.

"But my inspiration will be gone after dinner," Reagan whined.

Apparently Aunt Jeanie cared more about dinner being served on time than she did about Ray's inspiration.

I sat in between Nana and Santiago, figuring it was the best place to be, and Uncle Bob took his seat at the end of the table, where he seemed to be watching something on his phone. I wondered how long it would be until Aunt Jeanie yelled at him to put it away.

Sophia brought the food out to the table. We were having baked chicken, macaroni and cheese, broccoli, and corn muffins.

Dinner started off fine. Everyone was eating quietly until Francois, the only boy member of Triple Terror, decided that he needed to start a conversation. "Santiago, will you play Monster Mission with me after dinner?"

"Sure," Santiago said, and I knew immediately that he would regret it.

I loved to play video games, but I refuse to play them with Francois, because he always cheats and throws fits when he loses. If someone does better than him, he'll shut the game off. I nudged Santiago with my knee underneath the table and shook my head, but he only looked at me and smiled. He would have to learn the hard way.

"Excuse me," Aunt Jeanie said. "What mission?"

"Monster!" Penelope shouted.

Aunt Jeanie only wanted us to play educational games, not anything with scary stuff and violence. Monster Mission was about killing monsters, and if you lost, you were eaten by a three-headed dragon.

Aunt Jeanie put her fork down. "I've read about that game. It's awful. What is it doing in this house?"

Everyone looked at Uncle Bob.

He shrugged. "He wanted it, so I bought it for him. It's not that bad."

Uh-oh.

"Robert Maloney, you know I have a strict policy on the type of entertainment I allow the children to engage in! Do you want them to become homicidal maniacs and—" blah, blah, blah, insert cliché conversation about the dangers of kids playing violent video games.

I blocked Aunt Jeanie out and asked Santiago how his detective business was going until Nana stepped in.

"Oh, let it go, Jeanie. It's just a game."

Aunt Jeanie hated when Nana told her what to do. It was as if she always had to prove to Nana that she was a grown-up and not a little kid anymore. "Thank you, Mother, but this does not concern you."

"Then why are you having this conversation in front of all of us?" Nana asked.

Good point.

Aunt Jeanie sighed and picked her fork back up. "Anyway, Sanchez, Bex tells me that you run a business."

He nodded. "Yes, ma'am. Several business, but my main one is website design."

Even Uncle Bob looked impressed, and not many things impressed him. Santiago was super-smart, and a genius when it came to technological stuff. He went into detail, and Aunt Jeanie seemed very pleased.

I breathed a sigh of relief, but I should have known better. Santiago was actually making a good impression on my family and they weren't totally humiliating us. This was too good to be true.

"Bex, are you getting excited about Australia?" Aunt Alice asked.

She meant the trip she'd be taking me on, that summer. I nodded because my mouth was full of mac and cheese, but I was super-excited. I had even been doing a countdown on my calendar.

"Maybe Australia's too much," Aunt Jeanie said absently, as if she was talking to herself.

My heart raced. I hoped Aunt Jeanie was not going to ruin the trip for me. "What does that mean?"

Aunt Jeanie frowned. "Two weeks in a foreign country without me? I'm not so sure about it, anymore."

"But you promised me," I whined. "And I've been keeping up with my journal and getting better grades."

I didn't care if I sounded like a baby. Aunt Jeanie could not take the trip away from me. I'd been dreaming about it for months.

"Jeanie, what is your problem?" Aunt Alice asked. "You already said that she could come with me."

"So, I changed my mind," Aunt Jeanie said. "After all, Bex is my responsibility. I have to do what I feel is best for her. You're not the most reliable person, Alice."

Aunt Alice folded her arms across her chest. "What? Now you're afraid I won't take good care of her?"

I didn't need anyone to take care of me. I was practically an adult. Aunt Jeanie seemed to be trying to pick a fight with Nana and Aunt Alice and doing it at my expense.

Nana stood up from the table and headed toward the living room. "Jeanie, you told the girl she could go, so she's going."

"How come Bex only gets to go?" Priscilla asked. "I want to go to Australia, too. Aunt Alice likes Bex better than the rest of us."

"Yeah," the other kids said at the same time.

Aunt Alice sighed. "You guys know that's not true. In a few years, I'll take the rest of you on a cool trip."

"I wanna go now!" Francois shouted.

"I wanna do my dance!" Ray insisted. "My inspiration is back!"

"Nana has her shoes on the couch!" Penelope announced.

Aunt Jeanie rushed into the living room. "Mom!"

I decided to save Santiago by asking if we could be excused to go to the TV room. Aunt Jeanie, preoccupied with a rebellious Nana, gave us permission.

Santiago stood in front of the huge window that faced the Silverstein's house. Everything looked pitch black. An eerie glow shone out of one window.

"I wonder what's going on in that house at this very moment," he said. "I have to find out what they're hiding."

"They're probably not hiding anything. I think they're just strange."

Santiago stepped away from the window. "Nah, I think it's more than that. Hey, I bet if I can solve the mystery of

Scary Sherry and her family, then my detective agency will really take off. I've already gotten two more customers since I found out what happened to Gerald's iPod. I found a half-eaten black banana in there. I should have charged him extra for having to dig through that landfill."

It turns out that Gerald's iPod had fallen to the bottom of his locker and gotten buried under some stuff because Gerald was a slob. Paying someone ten bucks to dig to the bottom of your disgusting locker was probably not the best use of money.

"Bex, you have to get into that house," Santiago said. "Then you can really find out what their deal is."

"Santiago, I'm beginning to think that you need to put me on your payroll."

He frowned. "On second thought, you shouldn't go over there alone. Something could happen to you, and nobody would know. I'll figure something out."

I spent the rest of the night listening to Santiago rattle off theories about the Silversteins. Not my idea of a fun date, but I suddenly wanted to know what their deal was just so everyone could stop talking about them.

6

Slumber Party Terror

trembles in fear

Monday's rumor of the day was that Nelson Rodgers had fleas—which was ironic, because his father was a vet. The kid did spend a lot of time scratching. I figured he just had some kind of skin condition. But fleas? Gross!

Anyway, everyone spent the day treating Nelson as if he had the plague. Even his own friends wouldn't sit with him at lunch.

I hoped my friends wouldn't turn their backs on me if I happened to get caught up in some nasty rumor.

Friday night, I was super-stoked because my friends and I were having a slumber party. The four of us used to have slumber parties every Friday night, taking turns at different houses, but then all of a sudden my friends had decided that they wanted to do other things on Friday nights, and our slumber parties became scarce. That made me a little sad, but I would take what I could get.

After we pigged out on pizza, gave each other mayonnaise facials (Chirpy swore that mayo would do wonders for our skin), and had a rousing session of girl talk, it was time for my favorite part of the night—Scary Story Time!

I went to my desk and grabbed the flashlight. "It's my turn to tell a story, and I have a really good one."

"No," Lily-Rose said frowning. "You tell the most horrible stories. The last time, you gave me nightmares."

I took that as a compliment. "Good. That's the point of a scary story. Seriously guys, it's just a story. Stop being such cowards."

"Cowards, huh?" Marishca said. "If you're so brave, why don't you go and investigate a real haunted house?"

"Yeah," Lily-Rose and Chirpy agreed.

"W—what do you mean?"

Marishca folded her arms across her chest. "You know what I mean. I want you to go next door and look inside Scary Sherry's house."

My friends looked at me with smirks on their faces, but I wasn't about to let them make me look like some kind of chicken. "Fine. But there's no way I'm going alone. You guys have to come with me."

Lily-Rose climbed into her sleeping bag. "Yeah. Chirpy and Marishca, you go with her."

"You too, Lily-Rose. Remember there's safety in numbers," I said, trying to reassure my friends who looked as if they'd just seen a ghost.

"What good is numbers going to do us if Scary Sherry's mom casts a spell on us?" Lily-Rose asked. "She could turn us all into warty toads."

Chirpy suddenly stood up. "Let's do it. People have been telling different stories about Scary Sherry for years. Now we finally have a chance to put all these rumors to rest. There's a reason we have all gathered here tonight. Fate has brought us here."

Marishca rolled her eyes. "Zee whole zing is ridiculous."

I was with Chirpy. I was tired of wondering what was going on in that house. We needed to know the truth about this weird family, once and for all. Were they axe murderers fleeing the law? Were they witches? Ghosts? Vampires? I had to know.

"Put your shoes on, girls. The Tribe is getting down to the bottom of this mystery."

Lily-Rose and Marishca groaned as they grabbed their sneakers. I went into the garage to find flashlights for everyone, then we went out the side door of the garage.

Bunched together, we made our way over to the Silversteins' yard.

"Let's go through the back fence," Chirpy suggested. "I hope they don't have a dog."

"I haven't seen a dog," I told her.

I carefully lifted the latch and opened the gate that led to the backyard. The gate made a loud squeaking sound, and I was afraid they would hear us.

Quickly we tiptoed to the backyard and stooped beneath a large window.

"Look, zee curtains are open," Marishca said, pointing.

Sure enough they were, but it was hard to see inside from where we stood. All I could make out was candlelight.

Two men entered the living room.

I jumped. Mr. Silverstein and another man were each holding the end of something dark and long. Ms. Jillian had been right.

"W—what is that?" Chirpy asked.

"It looks like a body bag," Lily-Rose answered.

"A body bag?" Chirpy yelled, forgetting that we were supposed to be quiet. "Forget this. I'm getting out of here."

Chirpy backed away from the house, but she didn't notice the large bin behind her. It looked like those large containers the janitors used to collect trash.

She backed into it.

I lost my grip on my flashlight. The container toppled over and spilled.

On my hands and knees, I felt around on the ground for my dropped flashlight.

"Ow, somebody kicked me in the face!" Chirpy complained.

"Guys, quiet," I said. "We're supposed to be spying, here."

"What eez it, Bex?" Marishca asked.

"Hold on. I'm trying to see." Finally my hand landed on my flashlight, and I switched it on. I shone the light on the ground and the things that had fallen out of the bin.

I realized what they were and gasped. "Bones! Human bones!"

We totally forgot that we were supposed to be sneaking around and ran, screaming, back to Aunt Jeanie's. We let ourselves back in the garage door and stopped screaming, but we didn't stop running until we reached my room and locked the bedroom door.

I leaned against the door, trying to compose myself. "I can't believe it. Everyone was right about that family. They're murderers."

"Yeah, and that was a lot of bones," Lily Rose said as she snuggled into her sleeping bag. "They've killed more than a few people. Bex, you are living right next door to a living nightmare."

"What do I do?" I asked. "What if my family's in danger?"

Chirpy thought for a moment. "You have two options—you can either get the Silversteins to move, or call the police."

"I suggest the latter," Lily-Rose said. "If the police saw that dead body and all those bones, they'll arrest those sickos for sure."

Something didn't sit right with me, though. "What about Sherry? What would happen to her?"

I knew firsthand what it felt like to have a parent and prison and the other M.I.A. Even though I had family who loved me, I still felt like an orphan, sometimes.

"What about her?" Marishca asked. "You zink it is safe for her to live wiz murderers?"

That was a good point. The Silversteins were dangerous. Poor Sherry had to live there because they were her parents and she had no choice. Was she in danger, or was she in on it, too?

I had to call Santiago and tell him what we found.

"Whoa," he said. "That settles it."

"That settles what?" I asked.

"We know what they are. We just have to catch them in the act."

The night was long and restless. I kept waking up, thinking that the Silversteins were going to come after me in my sleep. It didn't help that Lily-Rose had woken up screaming several times from nightmares, and I had to keep Chirpy from smothering her with a pillow.

I was super-happy when the sun finally rose. We got dressed, and Sophia made us a big breakfast of pancakes and sausage.

Everything was going splendidly until the doorbell rang.

Sophia went to see who it was and then came back and whispered something in Aunt Jeanie's ear. If I hadn't known any better, I would have thought that she turned a little pale as she went to see who was at the door.

She opened the door. "Come in. Forgive us. We're having breakfast."

My heart stopped when Mr. Silverstein walked in with his hands behind his back. What was he hiding?

My friends and I all looked at each other and I knew what they were thinking. These were our final moments.

"Good morning. It seems that there was a little ruckus last night on our property. Someone knocked some things over."

"It wasn't us!" Lily-Rose blurted out way too fast.

Mr. Silverstein frowned. "Oh, okay. I found this and I thought it might belong to one of you. I just wanted to return it."

My throat tightened as Mr. Silverstein held up Chirpy's gold chain with a fairy charm. Her father had given it to her for a birthday gift.

Aunt Jeanie took the chain. "Does this belong to any of you girls?"

"I think it might be mine," Chirpy said in a tiny voice.

"How did it get next door?" Aunt Jeanie asked frowning.

"I have no idea," Chirpy replied. "It's a real mystery."

I expected Mr. Silverstein to yell at us about making a mess in his yard the night before, but he only smiled. "Well, I'll let you get back to your breakfast. Have a good day."

After Aunt Jeanie let him out, she came back to the dining room and gave us all the look of death. "Have you lost your minds? What were you doing in their yard?"

I shrugged. "Uh, I think we were sleep-walking—"

"Bex, stop it," Aunt Jeanie said. "I want you to stay off of those people's property. Do you understand me?"

"Yes, Aunt Jeanie."

"Yes, Mrs. Maloney," my friends replied solemnly.

Aunt Jeanie looked just a little bit afraid. What would she do if I told her what we had really seen?

7

Out of Control

—feeling frustrated ☹

Journal Entry #14

I have come to the conclusion that boys will always continue to confuse me. One minute they're dumping you, and the next, they're professing their undying love. I just don't get it. Aside from that, things at school are getting weirder and weirder.

Monday morning, the P.R.S. had struck again. I couldn't help but to take this rumor personally, since, well, it was about me.

Bex Carter and Harry Kline are deeply, madly in love.

When I heard about the rumor, I couldn't believe it, and I had to see it with my own eyes. I ran to the girls' bathroom, and sure enough, there it was, in huge red letters. I cringed when I saw it. Who on earth would write such a thing and why?

Everyone at Lincoln High knows that Harry Kline and I have a very complicated past.

In case you missed it . . .

Harry Kline was a boy I had really liked recently. He was running for class president, and we really wanted him to win. Ava G. suggested that he and I fake date in order to earn him some popularity votes. I liked Harry, and I thought he really liked me until he won the election and promptly started dating Ava T., who promptly dumped him and broke his heart. Since then, I had completely ignored the fact that he'd existed.

The last thing I needed was to be linked to Harry through some stupid rumor. Gossip might seem fun until it involves you.

Marishca caught up with me after second period. "I can't believe someone wrote zat."

"I know. We really need to get to the bottom of this."

"Santiago is going to be furious," she said.

"No," I said. "I think he'll understand that it's just a stupid rumor."

Marishca shook her head. "No, he's furious."

She pointed to Santiago storming down the hallway.

She was right. He did not look happy at all. Not only that, he was headed straight toward an unsuspecting Harry as he put in his locker combination.

"Yo, Kline. You have something to tell me?" Santiago called.

Harry glanced up, looking surprised, as I ran to put myself in between the two of them.

Harry pushed his glasses up on his nose. "Huh?"

"Is it true?" Santiago asked. "That the two of you are madly in love?"

Before I could open my mouth to tell him how ridiculous that was, Harry blurted out, "I love Bex with all my heart."

My jaw must have hit the floor. "What? Are you crazy?"

Harry turned to me. "It's true, Bex. I made a huge mistake. Will you forgive me and take me back?"

"No, she can't because she's going out with me, dweeb. You had your chance, and you blew it," Santiago said.

"Santiago," I said calmly. "I'll handle this. But, Harry, he's right. We're going out now."

Then Harry did something totally unsuspected. The sweet, gentle boy I had once known seemed like a totally different person. He stepped past me and right up to

Santiago. "Santiago, I challenge you to a duel. The winner takes the lady."

"Excuse me," I said. "You can't treat me like some kind of prize to win at a carnival. There's not going to be any duel. I'm never going out with you, Harry."

"That's right," Santiago agreed. "There's not going to be any duel, but there's going to be a major butt-whupping after school. Your prize will be a butt-whupping."

"Ooo," said a crowd of kids I hadn't noticed gathered around us.

Ava G. was one of them. "I didn't think I would ever see the day when two boys would be fighting over Bex Carter."

"Bex, you have to stop this," Lily-Rose said.

"Yeah," Marishca agreed. "Harry's going to get hurt, and Santiago's going to get in major trouble."

"I know. I know. Aside from that, we need to find out who's starting these rumors. This one person is causing all of these problems."

That afternoon, my cousin Francois burst into my bedroom, yelling at the top of his lungs. "That creepy girl from next door is at the door for you."

Scary Sherry. I cringed, hoping that she hadn't heard him.

When I got downstairs, Sherry was standing in front of the door, staring at the ground.

"Sherry?"

She looked up slightly, but her hair covered most of her face. "Hey, Bex. My room is all put together. I wanted to know if you wanted to come over and see it. You'll be the first friend I've had over."

I hadn't been even aware that Sherry had other friends.

So many thoughts raced through my mind. What if Sherry was only trying to lure me over because Mr. Silverstein was mad at us for being in his yard? What if I never made it out of that house alive? I was too young to die. I needed to call my friends and ask them what I should do.

"Uh, I would love to, but I have a lot of homework to do. You know Mrs. Conway gave us that killer social studies project. Maybe some other time."

Sherry grabbed my arm with her cold, clammy hand. "It'll only take a minute. Besides, I was watching you through my binoculars, and you were spinning a basketball on your finger."

Creepy!

"You were watching me through your binoculars?"

"Yeah, my bedroom faces yours. We can see each other all the time."

Just great. Note to self: Keep your curtains closed.

Now that I was officially weirded out, I really didn't want to go to her house, but I was stumped for a quick excuse.

At that moment, my wonderful baby sister came bounding down the stairs, and for once, I wished she would beg to tag along, like she always did. Even having an eight-year-old by my side would make me feel better.

"Hey, Ray," I said cheerfully. "I'm going next door to check out Sherry's new room. I bet you want to come."

She looked between Sherry and me a few times, and I braced myself. There was absolutely no telling what would come out of that girl's mouth.

"That's okay, Bex. I'm pretty busy, right now."

Thanks a lot, Ray.

I sighed and followed Sherry over to her house. Once I stepped inside, I realized that their house wasn't as weird as I thought it would be, although it wasn't exactly normal. Besides the fact that it was freezing, it looked like some kind of museum. Everything was antique and shiny. Aunt Jeanie would have died if she had seen their dining room— it was that fancy looking.

We walked up the long spiral staircase and into Sherry's room. I had expected to see a room with black walls, horror movie posters, and weird scary things.

I was quite shocked to see a room with bright aqua walls. Beautiful artwork and photographs of ocean scenes and animals lined the walls. Her headboard looked like a giant seashell.

"I like the ocean," she said quietly from behind me.

I almost jumped, but I was kind of getting used to her sneaking up on me. I could have sworn that she had just been standing somewhere else.

"Sherry, this is pretty cool," I said, and I meant it. "I had no idea that you were into the ocean like that."

"Yeah, I love the water. I would go swimming a lot more if I didn't sunburn so quickly."

Sherry was so pale, it was hard to believe that she ever went out in the sun.

"So you really like it?" she asked.

"Yeah. I do."

"You don't think it's lame?"

I admired a picture frame made out of sand dollars. "No way. It's awesome."

Sherry looked relieved. "Good. I thought it might be a little cheesy. That's why I didn't want you to see it the other day."

"Aw, who cares what I think? I just never pegged you as being an ocean enthusiast."

"There's a lot you don't know about me, Bex, but now that we're neighbors, we can really get to know each other."

I laughed nervously. "Yeah, that would be cool."

Sherry looked down at the ground and shrugged. "I hope you don't let what the other kids say about me get to you."

"What do you mean?" I asked, even though I knew.

"I know everyone calls me Scary Sherry. Most of the time, I don't mind, because it's just a stupid nickname, but some kids act like they're really afraid of me. There was even a rumor going around last year that if you said my name five times while looking into a mirror, I would come out of the mirror and haunt you."

I remembered that rumor. "I'm sorry, Sherry. Some people are just idiots."

I also knew that nicknames might seem fun to everyone except the person called by it. I've spent most of my school years being called Big Bex or Big Red because I was taller than everyone else.

"Yeah, but you don't believe those things about me, do you, Bex?"

"Of course not." I knew none of those rumors about Sherry was true, but I understood why people started them. She *was* strange. "Anyway, I really do have to go work on my homework now."

"Okay," Sherry said. "Maybe we can make up a secret code and send each other messages in the window, since we have a clear view of each other."

She was right. I could see my room, clear as day, from Sherry's bedroom window.

"Uh, a secret code?" I asked. "You have a cell phone, don't you?"

"Sure, but a secret code would be lots more fun." She went to her desk drawer, opened it, and pulled out a pair of binoculars. "Here, these are for you. Now we both have a pair."

I reluctantly took the binoculars from her and eased my way toward the door. "Let me think about that. I'll see you in school tomorrow."

"Okay," Sherry said, "and Bex? I'm glad we're neighbors."

I nodded and felt extremely guilty about all the things I had thought about Sherry and her family.

8

The Vampire
of Lincoln Middle

#bloodsuckers

I spent the morning trying to talk Santiago out of trying to beat Harry to a pulp, but he kept yelling about how Harry had challenged his manhood. I told him that middle school boys didn't have a manhood, and then he told me that *I* was challenging his manhood.

"I'd just let it go, Bex," Chirpy said. "There's no use in trying to understand boys when they get like that. They'll sort it out themselves."

The rumor of the day was found after third period.

Scary Sherry is a real live vampire.

Anybody with half a brain would know better than to give that rumor a second thought, but apparently most of the kids in my school were running around with forty-nine percent of their brains. They treated Sherry as if she was some kind of monster.

When they passed her in the hallway, they would make a cross with their fingers. Some kids even held on to the garlic bread that had been served in the cafeteria with the lasagna.

"This is so stupid," Chirpy said at lunch when Ava G. was going around, sprinkling some fancy bottled water all over the place. She claimed it was "holy water," AKA vampire repellant.

"Yeah," Lily-Rose agreed. "If Sherry were a real vampire, she wouldn't be able to go out during the day."

"That's not true," Ava said. "I saw a movie where there are now different types of vampires, and some of them can go out in daylight. Besides too many other clues are there. I mean, look at the girl. Does she look as if she ever looks in a mirror? We all know that vampires have no reflection."

"Ava, get out of here," I told her.

She smirked at me. "You're just in denial because you don't want to face the fact that you're living next door to a family of vampires. You'd better safeguard that house, Bex, or you and your family will be vampire bait. Toodles."

I rolled my eyes as she sauntered away.

Marishca looked at me. "Well, Bex, you said that you were in her house, and everything seemed pretty normal, right?"

"Yeah, I didn't see anything unusual."

"But we all saw those bones that night," Chirpy said. "Obviously they're not vampires, but there's something very, very wrong with that family."

Just then, Santiago plopped down at the table with his notepad. "I'm getting closer to finding out who this P.R.S is."

I looked at his notepad. He definitely had more written down than he had the other day. "Tell us what you got."

"The culprit is a girl. I finally found out what was being used to clean the writing off the walls—it's some kind of industrial cleaner purchased for the school board. One of the janitors is cleaning up the messages as soon as they find them. I spoke to Principal Radcliff, and he said they've tried finding out who is doing this by the surveillance cameras, but since it keeps happening in different bathrooms and there's so many kids going in and out, there's no way to tell. I've also come to the conclusion that this person has very messy handwriting, but they could just be trying to disguise their handwriting. And since all of the rumors have been about eighth graders, I'm sure that the culprit is in our class."

"So," Marishca said, "to sum it up—it's an eighth-grade girl wiz sloppy handwriting."

That wasn't very specific, but I didn't want to burst Santiago's bubble, since he had been working so hard.

He leaned in close and lowered his voice. "I do have a theory about who it could be."

"Who?" we all asked at the same time.

"Scary Sherry."

We all shook our heads. She was one of the last people who would do something like this.

"Why do you think it's her?" Lily-Rose asked.

"Think about it," Santiago said. "Kids have been spreading rumors about her for years. Maybe she just got tired of it and finally wanted to give everyone a taste of their own medicine."

I didn't believe that for a second. "But today's rumor was about Scary Sherry. Why would she start such an awful rumor about herself?"

"To throw everyone off," Santiago said. "It's actually a pretty smart move. And I don't think this rumor has been all that awful to her. Look."

Sherry had waltzed into the cafeteria with about eight kids trailing behind her. She waved to me as she passed, and I waved back.

"Whoa," Chirpy said. "When did Scary Sherry get a posse?"

Santiago closed his notebook. "It looks as if some kids in this school are actually obsessed with vampires. They've selected Sherry as their leader. I think they think she'll turn them into vampires, too."

Oh boy.

After school, I was on my way to soccer practice when I heard Harry Kline's voice. "Bex, wait up!"

I sped up. He was the last person I wanted to speak to. He had really hurt me, and it was bad enough that I had to see his face in the hallways every single day.

"I have somewhere to be, Harry," I said.

Harry caught up and stepped in front of me. "Hey, Bex. I just wanted to tell you that whoever wrote that rumor on the wall about us? Well, they were telling the truth—or at least, half the truth. I know I was the dumbest guy in the world for choosing Ava T. over you, but I was so wrapped up in having that perfect presidential image, I wasn't thinking straight. I miss all the fun we had together."

"Really? Didn't you have fun with Ava T.?"

He shook his head. "No, not at all. She's nothing like you."

"I could have told you that. She treated you like old moldy meatloaf, didn't she?"

He nodded sheepishly.

I didn't feel the least bit sorry for him. "Good! You deserve it. Good day."

I tried to step around him, but he grabbed my hands and got down on his knees. I looked around. Thankfully, the hallway was pretty much empty, because I was totally humiliated for Harry.

"Bex, please take me back. I promise, I'll treat you like a queen, and I'll never ever hurt you again." He started to kiss the backs of my hands.

I yanked my hands away from him. "Harry Kline, compose yourself. Have some dignity!"

But he didn't get up. He buried his face in his hands, and I sincerely hoped that he wasn't crying. "I don't care about that, Bex. Love can make a man act like a fool. I don't care how I look."

"Harry, I'm going out with Santiago, and I really like him. He would never do what you did to me. I know it's going to be hard, but you're just going to have to get over me."

He moved his hands away from his face and looked up at me. Ugh. He *was* crying. "I won't, Bex. I've liked you since the sixth grade, and I can't give up that easily. I'm going to have that duel with Santiago. I know we belong together."

Someone gasped behind me. I turned and saw only a flash of color.

Someone had been spying on us, and now they were on the run. Could it be the P.R.S.?

"Harry, hold on," I said as I took off after the privacy-invader. When I turned down the hallway, I didn't see anyone, but the door to the library closed. I ran inside.

All I saw was Ms. Roberts restacking books and a few kids working on computers. They seemed as if they had been there for a while.

The privacy-invader had eluded me. Had it been the rumor starter, or just someone being nosey? I hoped my conversation with Harry wouldn't end up on the bathroom wall the next day, because Santiago would flip. To make matters worse, I ended up being late to soccer practice, and I had to run two extra laps.

I seriously wished all this drama would blow over sometime soon.

9

Leaping to Conclusions

—feeling embarrassed ☹

Journal Entry #15

I don't know what's wrong with me. No matter what I do, it ends up being the wrong thing to do. Even when I think before I do things, it ends up being a disaster.

Thursday afternoon, while I should have been doing homework, I was distracted by movement going on at the Silverstein house. A big white truck had pulled up to the house, and several men began to unload it.

The first few things were large black duffel bags. I wished that I had X-ray vision so that I could tell what was inside them.

Then two men carried out something that looked like two large black body bags. I shivered.

The last thing brought out of the truck was a coffin. I might have been wrong about a lot of things, but I did know that there was only one use for a coffin—well, maybe two, if you believed that vampires were real, but I didn't.

I couldn't keep what I was seeing to myself. I had to call my friends and let them know.

"You have to call the police," Marishca said.

"She can't do that," Lily-Rose said. "I've changed my mind about calling the police. Have you actually seen a body or the Silversteins do anything wrong?"

"No, Lily-Rose," I said. "But they have a coffin and body bags. What do you think's inside? Candy?"

Lily-Rose sighed on her end of the phone. "I'm just saying. Calling the police is a big deal, and you have to live next door to these people. What if you make them really upset and become their next victim?"

She was right. I hadn't thought about that.

"Tell your aunt," Chirpy said. "She'll know what to do."

If I told Aunt Jeanie, she would definitely call the cops, and the entire neighborhood would know what was going on in less than five minutes.

Unfortunately, it only took one night for what I had seen at the Silversteins to spread through Lincoln Middle. The next morning, wild theories about Sherry were flying all over the school.

"How do they know?" someone asked from behind me as I got a drink from the water fountain.

"Huh?" I asked, turning around.

It was Sherry, who had sneaked up on me once again. "How do they know?"

"How does who know what, Sherry?"

"How do the kids know about what people were bringing into my house? The way I figure it, they could only have heard it from someone who lives in my neighborhood. Specifically, a next-door neighbor who goes to this school who can see the inside of my house from hers."

Busted. "Sherry, I—I didn't tell everybody, just my friends. I'm sorry—"

"That's all I needed to hear, Bex. And to think that I stayed up all night working on our secret signals. I thought you were cool, but you're not. I never want to speak to you again."

She walked away, and I wanted to call after her, but there was nothing I could say. There was nothing that I could possibly say that was going to make the situation right.

Saturday evening, Aunt Jeanie allowed Santiago to come over and watch movies with me, but that was only because Nana was going to be over to keep an eye on us and Sophia was to act as backup in case Nana fell asleep or drifted off. I hoped Nana wouldn't have one of her episodes. It scared me when she would forget things and wander away.

My aunt and uncle were getting all dressed up to go to dinner with some friends.

Santiago and I sat on the couch, feeling as if we were being interrogated.

"There is to be no kissing, touching, hand-holding. Santiago—"

At least she had finally gotten his name right.

"I expect you to behave like a perfect gentleman at all times. Tell him, Bob."

"If you touch my niece, I will break every last one of your fingers."

I sank deeper into the couch. Usually Uncle Bob was the only normal one around here. If he had lost it, all hope was gone.

Santiago nodded. "Yes, sir. I will keep my hands to myself."

Aunt Jeanie smiled as Uncle Bob wrapped a shawl around her shoulders. "We have a state-of-the-art surveillance system. We will see your every move. Have a fun evening."

"I'm sorry," I mouthed to Santiago. Between threats from my aunt and uncle, and the Brat Squad running around the house, I wondered why he was still there. If I were him, I would have run from the house screaming.

"Anyway," Aunt Jeanie said. "If you need anything, we'll be right next door."

I shot up from the couch. "Wait! What do you mean, right next door? At the Silversteins'?"

We had houses on both sides of us. *Please be talking about the other one. Please be talking about the other one.*

"Yes, the Silversteins'. They invited us over for dinner. Good night."

"You can't go over there, Aunt Jeanie," I pleaded. "I told you I saw things—body bags and coffins and things to hide dead bodies in. Please don't go." Aunt Jeanie and I had our issues, but I didn't want her or Uncle Bob to get hurt. They could not go over there.

Aunt Jeanie frowned. "Bex, weren't you the one who told us the other day that we should give them a chance before jumping to conclusions and judging them before we got to know them? You were absolutely right. I'm going to take your advice."

Santiago stood beside me. "Listen to her. They might be vampires."

He was so not helping the cause.

Just then, Nana came down the stairs, wearing a pink feather boa and way too much makeup on her face. The girls must have been giving her a makeover.

Nana laughed. "If anybody should be worried about anything, it should be the neighbors. Jeanie's mouth is more dangerous than a vampire's fangs."

Aunt Jeanie was not amused. "Mom, we'll be back in a couple of hours. Let Sophia know if you need anything. Don't let them watch any scary movies. They've got enough weird ideas in their heads."

Nana waved her away. "Yeah, yeah, yeah. I can take care of my own grandchildren."

Aunt Jeanie looked a little unsure, but she and Uncle Bob finally left.

I turned to Santiago. "We have to do something. I can't let anything happen to my family."

Santiago nodded. "Let's get those binoculars Sherry gave you and keep an eye on things. That way if we see something suspicious, we could at least warn your aunt and uncle."

"Okay." I ran upstairs to grab the binoculars and came back down to the TV room, which gave us a clear view of the Silversteins' dining room.

A few other couples were already there, and by seven o'clock, there were about ten people total, including the Silversteins.

After about fifteen minutes of Santiago and I passing the binoculars back and forth, we were bored out of our minds.

"How long are we going to watch them?" Santiago asked. "It just seems like a regular old dinner party to me."

"That's probably what they want. For everything to go normally and then *wham*! That's when they get you. When you least expect it. But I guess we can start the movie and then check back over in about ten minutes."

I let Santiago pick the movie, this time, although I felt Aunt Jeanie was right that we shouldn't watch scary movies—but she didn't allow them, anyway.

We started a comedy and were just getting into it when Santiago pointed over at the window. "Look."

We moved back over to the window. The lights had been dimmed. We could still see inside. Everyone was gathered around the large dining room table, and a woman in a black dress and white apron was serving plates covered with silver lids.

A man went around the table pouring water into glasses.

"What's happening now?" Santiago asked.

"Nothing. The food's being served."

Just then the lights went out in the Silversteins' dining room. Just the dining room. Lights were still on upstairs. Why did they only go out in that one room?

"Whoa," Santiago said. "Can you see anything?"

"Nothing. It's pitch black."

Just as I said that, the lights flicked back on. The maid was still standing there, holding a plate.

Everyone stood and pointed to one end of the table. They looked panicked. A woman was slumped over. Someone stood over her to check if she was still breathing, but from the look on everyone's faces I could tell that she wasn't.

Mr. Silverstein stood and waved his hands trying to get everyone to calm down.

"What's going on?" Santiago asked.

I told him everything that had happened. A man with a pipe and a trench coat stood and began to pace.

I couldn't believe it. "I don't get it. There's obviously a dead body at the table, and they're just sitting there. Why doesn't somebody call the police?"

How could my aunt and uncle just sit there, looking at a dead body, and not do anything?

"We have to call," I told Santiago.

He looked unsure. "Tell your nana first. She'll know what to do."

I left Santiago watching the dinner scene as I went to find Nana. She was in the kitchen with Sophia making ice cream sundaes.

"Nana, we have to call the police. Somebody's dead next door."

Nana frowned and put down the bottle of chocolate syrup that was in her hand. "How would you know that, Bex?"

What? I was telling her that there may have been a murder, and that was what she was worried about? "I was kind of watching through my binoculars, but only because I was worried about Aunt Jeanie and Uncle Bob."

Nana shook her head. "Bex, I'm sure if a murder had really taken place there, your aunt would be over here having a conniption. If a person goes looking for dirt, they're probably going to find it."

Nana was totally not being any help. What was wrong with everyone?

"I need to call the police," I told her.

"You are not calling the police. Now stop snooping in other people's homes, and go watch the movie with your friend. I'll bring your sundaes in a minute."

Reluctantly, I left the kitchen and went back to the TV room. Santiago was standing and backing away from the window.

"What's going on?" I asked.

"Bex, you won't believe it," Santiago said. "The lights when off again, and then the butler disappeared. We have to call the police."

"But Nana said not to."

Santiago dropped the binoculars. "Someone else could be dead by the time they get here, anyways. Let's go. We'll stop it ourselves."

I was glad that Santiago was feeling brave, because I felt terrified. What were we going to say to the Silversteins? What if we were their next victims?

Once we made it to the house, Santiago rang the doorbell and banged on the door. A moment later, Sherry answered. I hadn't seen her in the dining room all night. I wondered if she knew what was going on right in her own house.

"Bex, what are you doing here? Have you come to apologize?"

That was a weird thing to say when murders were taking place right in the dining room.

"Sherry, I totally owe you an apology, but right now there's an emergency happening right in your dining room," I said as Santiago and I pushed past her.

I ran into the living room.

Everyone froze, and Aunt Jeanie stood up. "Bex, what are you doing here?"

I ran and hugged her as tight as I could. "Aunt Jeanie, I'm so glad that you're still alive."

"Okay, Bex, that's sweet, but why wouldn't I be? What's going on?"

That was when I got a good look at the scene. Everyone was still sitting around the table.

The woman who had been slumped over in her chair was staring at me.

The butler, who was lying on the floor, was staring at me.

My heart shuddered, and I felt so stupid. "I just made a big mistake, didn't I?"

Mrs. Silverstein stood from her spot at the table. "Bex, what's going on?"

Everything I said was going to sound so silly, but I had some explaining to do. "We were kind of watching you through the window, and we thought that people were really being killed, so we were worried."

Mr. Silverstein nodded. "Bex, part of what we do for a living is hosting murder mystery parties on the weekend. We wanted to do one for some of the neighbors, just for fun so that we could get to know each other."

"Did you really think my parents were murderers?" Sherry asked from behind me.

I didn't even know how to answer that.

"Well, she had good reason to think that," Santiago said. "She's seen bones, and body bags, and coffins."

Mr. Silverstein chuckled. I was glad he could see the humor in this, because Aunt Jeanie looked as if she were going to explode at any moment.

"The *other* thing we do is make custom props for haunted houses and stage plays. A lot of those things end up being skeletons, coffins, and creepy-looking people."

"Oh," was all I could say.

"Bex?" Mrs. Silverstein asked.

"Yes?"

"If you had these suspicions, why didn't you just ask? Sherry could have explained everything to you."

I looked back at Sherry, who looked even more hurt than she had the other day at school.

"I tried to explain things to her, but she wouldn't listen," Sherry said. "Nobody wants to listen to what I have to say. They just want to believe what they want to believe. I hate that school, and I hate this neighborhood!" She ran from the room.

Aunt Jeanie and Uncle Bob left the table. "I'm so sorry about all this," Aunt Jeanie said. "I should take them home. It was a very nice evening before all of this. Thank you."

I wanted to apologize to Sherry, but I knew that she probably didn't want to hear anything I had to say—and besides that, Aunt Jeanie was dragging me from that house so fast that I thought my shoulder was going to come out of its socket.

She didn't say a word until we were back in the living room. "What on earth would possess you to do something like that? I mean, to accuse someone of murder—the worst thing you could ever do. What were you thinking?"

"I'm sorry, Aunt Jeanie. I saw some weird things, and I guess I just jumped to conclusions. We didn't mean any harm."

"Yeah," Santiago agreed. "We were just trying to look out for everyone."

Nana came into the room just then. "Oh, there you two are. Your sundaes have melted."

Aunt Jeanie turned her anger on Nana. "I thought you were supposed to be keeping an eye on them. Did you even know that they had left the house? They were next door, ruining a perfectly lovely dinner party."

Nana looked at me with her disappointed face. "Bex, didn't I tell you to leave those people alone?"

"You did. Aunt Jeanie, it's not Nana's fault." I hated when they fought.

Nana put her hands on her hips. "Just because someone might be a little weird doesn't make them bad people. You're weird. Are you a bad person?"

"Thanks, Mom, " Aunt Jeanie said. "It's getting late. I think you should just stay the night."

"Great," Nana said sarcastically. She hated spending the night at Aunt Jeanie's.

"Santiago, Mr. Maloney will take you home. Bex, you're grounded until further notice, and we have to think of some way for you to make things up to those poor people

10

Coming Clean

#keepingitreal

Journal Entry #16

I don't get why people say kids have no idea what stress is, because I'm totally stressing. Every time I turn around, there seems to be another problem. Yesterday, these three rumors surfaced in various bathrooms:

—Britney Jones and Whitney Lazaro are dating the same guy.

—Raven Dullop just got out of juvie.

—Marcus Blane is sharing our basketball secrets with our rival team.

Let me catch you up on all the drama that's going on right now all because of these rumors!

1. Ava is still trying to debunk rumors of her nose job. She even offered to take a lie detector test.

2. Piper has openly admitted to stuffing her bra because she was tired of everyone asking about it.

3. Willow is going extra hard on her vegetarian campaign to prove that she does not eat meat.

4. Nelson makes a very great effort to never scratch.

5. Everyone is more afraid of Sherry than they were before.

6. Henry and Santiago had decided to go on with their duel Friday afternoon in the park.

7. Britney and Whitney, who have been inseparable best friends since kindergarten, have vowed to never speak to each other again.

8. The basketball team is furious with Marcus and is threatening to kick him off the team.

My school is a mess!!!!

Monday morning, I had to set everything straight. I'd spent all of Sunday feeling like a total jerk. I hadn't even been able to talk to my friends because Aunt Jeanie had taken my phone away.

As soon as I got to school I began looking for Sherry, but I didn't have to look very far because she found me. The other kids in her new vampire clique stood behind her, and none of them looked happy.

I was just a tiny bit nervous. "Hey, Sherry. I was just looking for you. Can we talk?"

She nodded.

"Alone?" I asked. It would be a lot easier for me to talk to her without her band of followers glaring at me.

"Anything you have to say to me, you can say in front of my friends."

"Okay," I said. "I know that this doesn't make up for what I've done, but I want to apologize to you and your parents. I saw some strange things, and instead of asking and waiting to see what the story was first, I assumed some things that were very, very wrong, and for that, I'm sorry."

Sherry raised one eyebrow at me. "How could you think those things about my parents? They're honest hardworking people, just like your family. They'd never hurt anyone."

"I know, Sherry. Like I said, I'm really, really sorry and I'd like to make it up to you and your family."

"Will you tell the truth about what my family really does? People will believe it, if it's coming from you."

"Yes, I can do that." All I had to do was tell one person, and the whole school would know by lunch. Unfortunately, I didn't think this would make them treat Sherry any differently. We had been calling her Scary Sherry long before any talks of body bags and coffins.

Finally, Sherry gave me a small smile. "Thanks, Bex. I guess I'll see you around."

I did the best I could, but I was very sad to learn that bad news travels a lot faster than good news. It seemed as if people were determined to believe the horrible things about Sherry's family rather than believe the good parts.

That evening Aunt Jeanie sent me over to the Silversteins with a tray of cookies.

"You apologize and do anything that you have to do to make this right," she said, before slapping me on the butt and pushing me toward the door.

"Okay, okay," I said.

My knees shook as I rang the Silversteins' doorbell. I didn't know how they were going to react to me. They hadn't seemed terribly angry on the night of the dinner party, but now that they'd had time to think things over, were they going to be upset with me?

Mr. Silverstein answered the door. "Hello, Bex. Come on in."

I breathed a sigh of relief. So, he wasn't angry.

"Sherry isn't here. She's at her acting class."

"Sherry takes acting classes?" I asked. "Cool." I handed him the tray of cookies. "Here. These are for you."

Mr. Silverstein took the plate. "Mmm. Chocolate chip cookies, our favorite. My wife and I like to nibble on snacks while we work, so this is perfect timing. Come on down to the basement."

I swallowed hard. "The—the basement?"

"Yes, we're working on some props down there. Would you like to see?"

Was this all a ploy to get me to go down to their basement, so they could extract their revenge on me? Everyone knows that terrible things always happen in the basement. "Um, sure."

I followed Mr. Silverstein and the tray of cookies down to the basement, where we found Mrs. Silverstein sitting at a table, painting.

She saw me and smiled brightly. "Hey, Bex, what a pleasant surprise."

"Bex brought us some cookies," Mr. Silverstein said to his wife as he sat across from her at the table. He placed the tray in the middle of the table.

Mrs. Silverstein reached for a cookie. "Perfect. I could use a bite to eat right now. Pull up a chair, Bex."

I grabbed a chair and pulled it to the table as I took in the basement. If I hadn't known better, I would have been totally creeped out by what I saw. Puppets hung from the ceiling. Skeletons stood against the walls. There was even a shelf of evil-looking dolls.

"What are you guys working on?" I asked.

"We are making a couple of ventriloquist dummies for a magician," Mr. Silverstein answered.

"Cool," I said. "Anyway, I don't want to keep you from your work, I just wanted to come by and apologize for ruining your dinner party and thinking that you were doing something wrong, when you were only doing your job."

Mrs. Silverstein carefully painted the lips of her dummy. "It's fine. We're in an unusual line of work and get a lot of weird stares and stories started about us. We're used to it."

"But that doesn't make it right," I said. "I don't know how I could, but I'd like to make it up to you."

The Silversteins looked at each other.

Mr. Silverstein cleared his throat. "Well, we could always use an extra hand with our mystery dinner theater. Sherry is a huge help, but sometimes she wants to do other things on the weekends. You can fill in for her and maybe play one of the parts."

I didn't know anything about mystery dinner theatre except for what I had seen on some TV shows, but it seemed easy enough. "I could do that."

Mrs. Silverstein took a cookie from the plate. "Thanks for coming by, Bex. It was big of you to apologize. We're glad that Sherry has a friend like you."

I couldn't really take that kind of credit because I hadn't been a good friend to Sherry at all. I left the Silversteins with the promise that I would help them when they needed me, and I promised myself that I would make things up to Sherry so that she could trust me and look at me as someone she could be friends with. After all, we lived right next door to each other. It would be nice to have someone right next door to hang out with, and this time, I didn't care what any of the other kids thought.

11

Who Done It?

#TeamSleuth

"All right," Santiago said. "We have to get down to the bottom of this, once and for all."

I was sitting with my friends at lunch, and we were desperately trying to figure out who was starting these rumors. This nonsense had to come to a stop so that Lincoln Middle could go back to its normal self. Well, it's never been really normal, but it had been more normal before all these rumors began to fly.

Santiago took out his trusty notepad and began to write a list of names.

1. Sherry

2. Raven Dullop

3. Harry Kline

"I already told you why I think it's possible that Sherry would have started a rumor about herself. Raven—maybe she wants everyone to think that she went to juvie so we'll be afraid of her."

Raven was this cool mysterious girl who had shown up a couple of months ago, wearing combat boots and all black. The front part of her hair was dyed lavender. We didn't know much about her, but she didn't seem like the type to be writing rumors in bathrooms.

"Harry Kline—"

"I thought you said it had to be a girl," Chirpy said, interrupting.

"I did," Santiago answered. "But I've been thinking. Maybe he puts on a dress and a wig and goes in there and writes those rumors."

"Why would he do that, Santiago?" I asked.

He shrugged. "I don't know. I'm grasping at straws, here." He pushed his notepad across the table. "I give up."

"We can't give up," Marishca said. "Zees person must be stopped, and zay will only stop when zay are discovered."

"Don't worry. We'll figure it out," I said, trying to reassure my friends.

During last period, Principal Radcliffe had called an emergency eighth-grade assembly. Apparently he had gotten tired of all the drama, too.

He looked frazzled as he ran his hands through his salt-and-pepper hair. I couldn't blame him. This wasn't the first assembly he'd had to call because of the insanity going on in the eighth grade.

"Ladies and gentlemen, settle down, settle down," he said as he stood behind the podium.

Within seconds, everyone was seated and quiet.

He cleared his throat. "It's no secret that we have a huge problem with rumors and gossiping. Someone thinks it's funny to write things about their classmates on the stalls of the bathrooms. Not only is spreading gossip a problem, so is defacing school property. We will not be leaving this room until we find out who is responsible for this."

Everyone looked around. The Phantom-Rumor-Starter was somewhere in that auditorium.

"If anyone has anything to say, please come to the mic," Principal Radcliffe said. He always liked for us to have open discussions. I guessed that was a good thing.

Santiago stood and made his way to the front of the auditorium. "Principal Radcliffe, if I may. I've been following this case carefully."

Principal Radcliffe nodded, but he didn't look very impressed.

Santiago continued, "Let's go back to the beginning. How did this all start?"

"I remember," Miranda said, standing. "I was checking my lip gloss in the mirror one morning when someone told me that Piper stuffs her bra." She looked at the ground. "I guess I kind of spread it. Sorry, Piper. Later that day, we discovered the rumor written in the stall."

If only my bladder had been stronger and I could have waited a minute longer and used another stall, or if only I could have read those words in my head. Still, it wouldn't have stopped the P.R.S. from spreading more rumors.

"Who was it who told you that, Miranda?" someone asked.

She thought for a moment. "I'm not sure. I always thought that the voice sounded familiar."

I sank down into my seat. *Please don't remember, Miranda. Please don't remember.*

"Come to think of it," Miranda said. "It sounded exactly like Bex Carter."

Principal Radcliffe nodded as if he knew I had to be involved.

Everyone turned to me, and I stood up. "No way. You can't just go by that. A lot of us have voices that sound alike."

Miranda shook her head. "No, Bex. You talk enough for me to know what your voice sounds like."

She had a lot of nerve, to be saying that. She talks more than anybody.

This needed to end, right then and there. "Okay, okay. I read the rumor out loud, but that's all. I swear, I didn't write it. I had no idea that Miranda the world's biggest gossip was standing right there, and she took it and ran before I could explain."

"Let's refrain from name-calling," Principal Radcliffe chided.

Santiago pointed at Miranda. "But you are the world's biggest gossip. Maybe you wrote the rumors so you'd have something to talk about. Maybe your gossip well was running dry, so you had to create your own."

Miranda clutched her chest and looked truly offended. "Excuse me? I never make up gossip. Any news that I spread is news that I've heard from someone else. It's true and reliable. Hey—I just remembered something."

Everyone stared at Miranda, waiting.

"The day the first rumor started, I saw Natasha Del Rio coming out of that stall. Maybe she wrote it."

All eyes went to Natasha, who was already shaking her head. "I've never written anything in a bathroom stall, I promise. I only went in there because I really had to go, and all the others were full."

I believed her, because the same thing had happened to me.

Just then, Ms. Waters, the assistant principal, walked across the stage and whispered something into Principal Radcliff's ear. He covered the mic with his hand and nodded as she spoke.

When Ms. Waters walked away, he spoke into the mic. "The guilty party has been identified. You may all go back to class."

Half of the auditorium groaned because they didn't want to go back to class, and the other half wanted to know who it was.

Principal Radcliffe refused to spill the beans. "The persons responsible for all this will issue a public apology tomorrow during the morning announcements."

After that, we were sent back to our classes. I was happy that whoever had started all this was finally caught, but unfortunately the damage had already been done.

The next morning, two tiny sixth-grade girls stood on the news, both shakily holding a piece of paper in their hands.

The girl on the right had short brown hair and freckles. "Dear eighth graders, we sincerely apologize for all the trouble we have caused you. My friend and I thought that the rumors would be good payback."

Payback? What had we ever done to them?

The other girl took over. "We got really fed up with being skipped in the lunch line, shoved into lockers, called runts, and all the flat-out disrespect."

Oh, yeah. That. Who would have thought sixth graders were responsible for all this? Those sneaky little runts!

Ragging on sixth graders was like a rite of passage. Every student had gone through it at some point, so I guess we never saw it as that big a deal. If they'd wanted to get us back—boy, had they.

"Two weeks ago, some eighth grade boys taped a sixth grader to his locker," the girl continued. "We just wanted to teach you a lesson. We want to be respected. Being the little fish in a big pond is hard enough."

Principal Radcliffe came on to remind everyone that that type of behavior wouldn't have been tolerated. I think we all felt pretty silly, knowing that our lives had been turned upside-down by a pair of sixth-grade girls.

After school, Santiago was waiting for me by my locker as usual. "Are you coming to the park?" he asked as I approached.

"Are you still thinking about this stupid duel? Seriously? You know that stuff about Harry and me was made up by sixth graders."

Santiago narrowed his eyes. "It doesn't matter. Harry's still walking around professing his undying love for you. It's disrespectful, and I have to set him straight."

I groaned. "But Santiago, it's so stupid. I'm going out with you, not Harry. Who cares what he says? There's no reason for you to fight him."

"You don't get it," Santiago said. "It's the principle. I have to do this."

"Santiago, I will not date a fighter. If you go through with this duel, we're through."

He looked crushed, and I felt a little guilty. "You would break up with me over that?"

"Yes. You know that you would pulverize Harry. That kid's never been in a fight in his life. Please, call it off."

Santiago thought for a moment and sighed. "Fine. I was way off about the P.R.S., wasn't I?"

I laughed. "We all were. No one would have guessed that."

We headed out of the building.

"So what's your next case?" I asked.

"I think I'm hanging up my detective hat. It takes up too much time. I'm thinking of becoming a therapist for kids who have been traumatized by this rumor fiasco."

"Santiago . . ."

"Hear me out. I could charge twenty bucks a session just to act like I'm listening—"

I let him talk. I loved the way he came up with ideas off the top of his head and got so excited about them, even though some of them were ridiculous.

As we walked, I spotted Sherry and her vampire-loving friends sitting on the steps. I gave her a small wave, and she waved back. If anything, at least she had gained a few friends out of this, even if they were a little weird.

Life Lesson from Bex:

Get all the facts before you spread information. What seems funny to you may actually hurt someone else. Also, stay out of cursed bathroom stalls!

Join my mailing list to be notified of sales and upcoming releases!

http://eepurl.com/HappH

Look out for Bex Carter #7:My B.F.F. (Bogus Fake Friend) coming soon!!!

Other books in the Bex Carter Series:

#1: Aunt Jeanie's Revenge

#2 Winter Blunderland

#3 All's Fair in Love and Math

#4 The Great "BOY"cott of Lincoln Middle

#5 Love, Politics, and Red Velvet Cupcakes

#6 So Scandalous

Don't Miss Out on Bex's earlier adventures:

The Fairylicious Series

#1 Fairylicious

#2 Delaney Joy: Fairy Exterminator

#3 Bex Carter: Fairy Protector

#4 D.J. McPherson: Fairy Hunter

#5 Bex Carter: Middle School Disaster and Reluctant Fairy Hunter

Made in the USA
San Bernardino, CA
13 January 2017